W9-ATF-366

Hi! I'm Darcy J. Doyle, Daring Detective,

but you can call me D.J. The only thing I like better than reading a good mystery is solving one. When Darla Wiggins said *she* was the best detective at Bayside Elementary, I had to do something about it. Let me tell you about the Case of the Bashful Bully.

Books in the Darcy J. Doyle,

Daring Detective series:

Darcy J. Doyle
Daring Detective

The Case of the
Bashful Bully

Linda Lee Maifair

ZondervanPublishingHouse
Grand Rapids, Michigan

A Division of HarperCollinsPublishers

The Case of the Bashful Bully
Copyright © 1994 by Linda Lee Maifair

Request for information should be addressed to:
Zondervan Publishing House
Grand Rapids, Michigan 49530

ISBN 0-310-43281-2

All rights reserved. No part of this publication may be reproduced, stored in a retrieval system, or transmitted, in any form or by any means—electronic, mechanical, photocopy, recording, or any other—except for brief quotations in printed reviews, without the prior permission of the publisher.

Edited by Dave Lambert
Interior design by Rachel Hostetter
Illustrations by Tim Davis
Cover design by Anne Huizenga

Printed in the United States of America

94 95 96 97 98 99 / ❖ OP /10 9 8 7 6 5 4 3 2 1

For my niece,
Tessa Conaway

CHAPTER 1

I'm Darcy J. Doyle. Some of my friends call me Darcy. Some just call me D.J. If I keep on solving important cases, pretty soon everyone will be calling me Darcy J. Doyle, Daring Detective. It's only a matter of time.

My last big case started the day we got a new boy in our class. "Boys and girls," Miss Woodson said, standing in front of the class with the new boy beside her. "Say hello to Ryan Nelson."

We each said hello in our own way:

"Hi!"

"Hey, Ryan!"

"Yo!"

The new boy stared at the floor.

Miss Woodson put a hand on his shoulder. "Ryan just moved here from Chicago."

The class was impressed.

"Wow! Chicago!"

"Really?"

"Bet you're a Cubs fan, huh, Ryan?"

Ryan still didn't answer. *Seems awfully shy*, I thought.

"I'm sure you will all do what you can to make Ryan feel welcome at Bayside Elementary." Miss Woodson looked around the room. She smiled at Josh Henderson. "Why don't we give Ryan the seat next to you, Josh?" she said. "You can show him around today."

"Sure thing, Miss Woodson," Josh said.

I wasn't surprised that Miss Woodson had chosen Josh. Josh is the sort of kid adults call "dependable." Everybody likes Josh. If anybody could make a bashful kid like Ryan Nelson feel welcome, it would be Josh Henderson.

I wasn't surprised when Josh took Ryan to the library and helped him pick out a book for his book report. I wasn't surprised when Josh led Ryan through the cafeteria line and warned him about the Noodle Surprise. I wasn't even surprised when Josh let Ryan have first shots with the class basketball at recess.

But even a daring detective gets surprised sometimes. I was as astonished as everybody else when Ryan Nelson punched Josh in the mouth on the basketball court, knocking him down and then sitting on top of him.

"It's none of your business!" Ryan shouted, waving a fist in Josh's face.

Josh tried to wriggle free. "I — I was just trying to be — friendly."

"I don't want you to be friendly!" Ryan shouted. "I want you to leave me alone! I want everybody to — "

He didn't get to finish. Our physical education teacher, Mr. Weis, grabbed him by the back of the collar and hauled him up away from Josh. "Break it up!" he hollered.

Josh stood up and brushed himself off. "Honest, Mr. Weis," he said, carefully feeling his jaw. "I was just trying to talk to him and he socked me."

"We'll discuss it inside," Mr. Weis said. He took both boys into the building. Most of the fifth and sixth graders stood around, staring at the door where they had disappeared.

"What was *that* all about?" Leon asked.

Nobody knew.

"He seemed so quiet," Cheryl said. "Shy, even."

Everybody agreed.

11

"Wonder what *his* problem is," said Matt, and we all shrugged and nodded, fifth and sixth graders alike.

"*I* could find out — if I wanted to," Darla Wiggins boasted. "Being a trained reporter."

Darla was the editor of the *Bayside Bugle*, our school newspaper. Sometimes she acted like that made her more important than the rest of us.

Darla was also a sixth grader. So it was sort of a matter of fifth-grade pride when my best friend Mandy Thompson said, "So could D.J."

Darla gave her one of those looks sixth graders like to give fifth graders. "Who?" she said, even though she knew very well who Mandy was talking about.

Mandy thumped me on the back. "Darcy J. Doyle, Daring Detective," she told Darla. "D.J. can solve any mystery."

I was happy that Mandy had gotten the name right. And I was glad she believed in me. But I had a funny feeling about this particular mystery. Especially when I saw the gleam in Darla Wiggins's eye.

"Oh, really, D.J.?" Darla said. She gave me a challenging grin. The whole sixth grade grinned with her.

The whole fifth grade stared at me. "Uh, sure," I said. I remembered what Darla had said herself. "If I wanted to."

Darla put her hands on her hips and glared into my eyes. "I bet I can find out more than you can."

"Darla! Darla! Darla!" the sixth graders started to chant.

"Darcy! Darcy! Darcy!" the fifth graders replied.

I didn't see any way out of it. The whole fifth grade was counting on me. And I really didn't want to see a smart aleck like Darla Wiggins win. I crossed my arms over my chest and gave her my most confident Daring Detective smile.

"I bet you can't," I said.

CHAPTER 2

The whole fifth grade was anxious to help me with my investigation. All afternoon, kids came over and whispered suggestions in my ear.

"Maybe he ran away from home."

"Maybe his family is hiding from somebody. Like in the movies?"

"Maybe his parents just got a divorce."

"Maybe he's really an alien — you know, from another galaxy."

I wrote all of the suggestions — except the one about the alien — in my notebook. And I kept an eye on Ryan Nelson all afternoon, although there wasn't much to see. From the time he came back from the principal's office until it was time to line up and go home, he sat slumped forward in his seat, leaning on his elbows, staring at the top of his desk. He didn't look very happy.

When our row went to get our book bags from the coatroom, I asked Josh, "Why did Ryan Nelson sock you?"

He shrugged. "Who knows? I was just talking to him — or trying to, he's so shy and quiet. I thought maybe I could get him to say something if I asked him a few questions."

"What sort of questions?" I asked.

"You know," Josh said. "The sort of stuff you'd ask anybody who was new in school. How he likes Bayside. If he misses Chicago. Where he lives. Why they moved here. What his mom and dad do. Stuff like that."

Writing fast, I scribbled the questions in my notebook. "What did you find out?" I asked.

Josh touched his puffy lower lip with the tips of his fingers. "I found out I shouldn't ask questions."

That didn't exactly make me anxious to talk to Ryan Nelson. But I reminded myself that I was supposed to be Darcy J. Doyle, *Daring Detective*. So when we were dismissed, I dodged through the crowd in the hallway, trying to catch up to Ryan.

Darla Wiggins got to him first. "I'm the editor and star reporter for the *Bayside Bugle*," she told Ryan. "You know, our school newspaper? We do an article on all the new kids here at Bayside. I was wondering . . ."

As Darla talked, Ryan's expression got angrier and angrier, and then he clenched his fists. For a second or two, I thought he was going to slug her. Darla must have thought so,

too. She took a couple of steps backward. "I — I was just wondering," she said, trying again.

Ryan didn't give her a chance to finish. "I hate newspapers," he growled. "And reporters." He shoved his fists into the pockets of his jacket and stomped away.

I decided to interrogate Miss Woodson instead. I wrote in my notebook: *Hates newspapers and reporters.* Then I went back to the classroom to get my library book.

I took my time, rooting through the books and papers in my desk. "Wasn't that something — about Josh and Ryan?" I said to Miss Woodson.

She looked up from the spelling tests she was grading. "Yes," she agreed. "It was very unfortunate."

Actually, I'd been thinking it was kind of exciting. "Do you know very much about Ryan Nelson?" I asked.

Miss Woodson arched one eyebrow at me. "A little," she said.

For some reason, the way she said it made me feel funny. "I, uh — I bet it's a lot different for him here. I mean, after Chicago," I hinted. "I bet they had a real good reason for moving to Bayside."

Miss Woodson got up from her desk and walked over to put her arm around my shoulders. "If you were a new student, in a new town, you wouldn't want your teacher talking about you behind your back, would you, Darcy?"

I hadn't been thinking about how Ryan might feel. "Not really," I admitted.

Miss Woodson smiled. "So you can understand why I can't discuss Ryan Nelson?"

Daring detectives don't like it when their investigations come to a dead end, but I knew

Miss Woodson was right. I nodded. "I understand."

"Good," Miss Woodson said. She went back to her desk.

I stuffed my library book into my book bag and headed toward the door.

"Darcy?"

I turned around. "Yes, Miss Woodson?"

"One thing I can tell you."

Aha! I was about to get a really big clue. I hoped it was something Darla Wiggins wouldn't know about. "What's that, Miss Woodson?"

What Miss Woodson told me didn't help my case a bit, but it did give me something to think about. "Ryan Nelson doesn't need a detective right now, Darcy," she said. "What he needs is a friend."

CHAPTER 3

Mandy was waiting on my front step when I got home. "Where'd you disappear to?" she asked.

"I was working on the Ryan Nelson case," I told her.

She smiled excitedly. "What'd you find out?"

I plopped down beside her. I hadn't found out a single thing, but I hated to admit that to Mandy, who thought I could solve any mystery. "Not much," I said. I dug through my backpack and found the candy bar I'd saved from lunch. "Want some?"

She didn't get to answer. My faithful blood-hound, Max, came barreling around the corner of the house. He put a paw on each of my shoulders and licked my face. "Good old Max," I grunted, holding the candy bar away from him with one hand and shoving him backward with the other. "He always knows when I'm working on a new case."

Mandy laughed. "I think he just knows when you have a new candy bar."

I gave Mandy one of my looks. "All good detectives expect an advance payment when they take on a new job." I broke the candy bar into three pieces. I gave one to Max and one to Mandy.

"Well, I've already earned *my* advance payment," she said. "I found out something about Ryan Nelson for you."

I didn't want to look desperate for clues — even though I was. I stuffed what was left of the candy bar into my mouth and let Max lick the chocolate from my fingers. Then I pulled my notebook and pencil out of my book bag. "What did you find out?" I asked.

She licked the chocolate off her own fingers, one at a time. Max grumbled in her direction. Good old Max. He was just as anxious as I was to hear what Mandy had to say.

"Ryan Nelson lives on Kennedy Boulevard," she said at last. "In a brick house with white shutters. Right across from Milton Park."

Mandy had found out more than I had. But I didn't bother pointing that out to her. "How do you know that?" I asked.

She looked pretty pleased with herself. "I saw him talking to Darla Wiggins after school," she said. "Then he started walking down Fairmont. I didn't see you around anywhere, so I followed him home."

I told her what had happened between Darla and Ryan. "It seems like he gets mad when anybody tries to ask questions," I said.

"Then how are you going to ask him anything?" Mandy asked.

I had no idea. "No problem," I told Mandy. "A good detective knows how to handle a hostile witness."

Mandy made a face. "How to do what?"

"You know," I explained. "How to talk to somebody who doesn't want to talk to you — without him bopping you in the nose."

"Too bad good detectives don't know how to handle their dogs," Mandy said. She pointed at Max.

He had his whole head inside my book bag. I grabbed his collar and pulled him back out. "I already have my notebook, boy," I told him.

Mandy laughed. "I don't think he was looking for your notebook in there, Darcy."

I looked her in the eye. "Of course he was," I said. "He knows we'll need it when we go to see Ryan Nelson."

Mandy took Max's leash and waited while I got Mom's permission to go to Ryan's. Mandy had to be home for her piano lesson by four, so she could walk with me only as far as her house.

While we walked, I told her about all the theories the kids had about Ryan Nelson — even the one about the alien.

We stopped at Mandy's front sidewalk. "You better be careful, Darcy," she warned me. "You know what happened to Josh Henderson."

"I'm not worried," I said, trying to sound daring. "I've got a trained attack animal with me."

Mandy's neighbor's cat chose that particular moment to hop up on the porch rail and hiss at Max, who let out a yelp and dove headfirst into the hedges in Mandy's front yard. It took all my strength to pull him back out again.

Mandy shook her head at my trained attack animal. "Yeah, right," she said.

CHAPTER 4

By the time Max and I got to Kennedy Boulevard, I was sort of hoping Ryan wouldn't be home. I kept thinking about Josh touching his puffy lip and saying, "I learned I shouldn't ask questions." But there Ryan was, sitting on his front porch having some cookies and milk.

Max took off across Ryan's front lawn, dragging me behind him. He cleared the front steps in one jump and held out his paw to Ryan. Good old Max. He's never afraid to interrogate a witness, hostile or not.

The witness held his bag of peanut-butter

cookies over his head. He looked like he wanted to run, but good old Max had him cornered.

"Max won't hurt you," I told Ryan. "He just wants to say 'hello.'"

Ryan grinned. "To who — me or my bag of cookies?"

I grinned back. "Both."

Ryan held out a half-eaten cookie. "Hello, Max," he said. Max barked his hello and grabbed the cookie. "Nice dog."

Ryan didn't sound like a bully who likes to bop kids on the school playground. "I'm Darcy," I said. "I'm in your class."

"Yeah, I know." Ryan stared at me for a couple of seconds, as if he was trying to make up his mind about something. Finally, he held out the bag. "You want a cookie?" he offered. "A glass of milk maybe?"

I couldn't pass up the chance to get inside Ryan's house. Maybe I could meet his mother or father, or at least find out more about him. "Sure," I said.

But I didn't get inside after all. He went in to get the milk himself, then came back out and handed me the glass. "Mom's taking a nap," he explained. "She works nights. At the Crestwood Diner. Grandma isn't home right now."

He scratched Max on the top of the head. "He know any other tricks — besides shaking hands?"

I broke off a piece of my cookie. "Speak, Max," I said.

"WOOF! WOOF!" Max gobbled down the piece of cookie.

I broke off another piece. "Sit up!"

Max sat up and waved his paws at the cookie in my hand. I tossed it high in the air. He caught it.

I held up a big chunk. "Roll over, Max!"

This wasn't one of Max's best tricks. He always got his feet sort of tangled up when he did it. And even I had to admit that sometimes it looked pretty silly. But Ryan didn't laugh. "Wow!" he said. "Smart dog."

"Yeah," I started to brag, "Max helps me with all my —" I stopped just in time. I had a feeling Ryan Nelson wouldn't like detectives any more than he liked reporters. "I was just taking him to the park. For a walk. Want to come along?"

Ryan had a nice smile. "Sure!" he said.

Ryan went inside to leave a note for his grandmother. While I waited, I suddenly remembered what Miss Woodson had told me: *Ryan Nelson doesn't need a detective right now. He needs a friend.*

My cookies and milk felt like a hard lump in my stomach when Ryan came back out and smiled at me again. "Let's go!" he said.

We had a good time in the park. We skipped stones across the pond. We had a race from the swings to the popcorn stand. We chased Max, who chased two squirrels and a rabbit and an old potato-chip bag and never caught any of them. And I didn't ask Ryan a single question.

"Some of the kids are going to play baseball on Saturday morning," I told him. "You want to come?"

Ryan looked nervous all of a sudden. "I can't," he said. "Mom and I have to go to . . ." He stopped. "We go away on Saturdays," he said.

My daring detective mind was curious. *Where do they go on Saturdays?* I wanted to know. *And why does he look so upset about it?* But I didn't ask. "That's OK," I said. "Sometimes we play after school, too. You can come then."

He smiled, but his smile didn't last very long.

When we got back to his house, Darla Wiggins was helping Ryan's grandmother get her groceries out of the car. "So Ryan and his mother are living with you now, Mrs. Anderson?" Darla was saying. "Why did they —"

I knew what she was going to ask, but she didn't get to ask it. Ryan rushed over and grabbed the grocery bag from her hands. "What are you doing here?" he snapped. "Nobody here wants to talk to you."

His grandmother seemed surprised and embarrassed. "Ryan! This nice young lady was just trying to help me."

Ryan looked at Darla the way you might look at a worm in an apple you've just bitten into. "No, she wasn't, Grandma. She just wants something exciting to write about in that newspaper of hers. She's just like all the others."

Carrying the grocery bag, Ryan stomped past Darla and headed for the front door. I felt like a worm myself when he turned around and said, "I'm sorry, Darcy. Guess this isn't a good time. But you and Max can come back again."

"Yeah, sure, Ryan," I started to say.

But Darla interrupted. "Well, well, well," she said. "If it isn't Darcy J. Doyle, Desperate Detective!"

Ryan peered at Darla over the top of his grocery bag. "Who?" he asked.

"Ryan, I —" I tried again.

Darla was real good at interrupting. "Darcy's famous at Bayside Elementary, Ryan," she told him. "The fifth graders say she can solve any mystery. That's why they asked her to find out about you."

I was glad Ryan had his arms full of groceries, although I wouldn't have blamed him much if he'd clobbered me. "Ryan, in the park . . . I wasn't trying to . . ." It was impossible to explain.

And Ryan wasn't listening anyway. He looked more hurt than angry. "Just stay away from me, Darcy J. Doyle," he said.

CHAPTER 5

I called Mandy as soon as I got home. "I'm taking myself off the case," I told her.

"But Darcy!" she protested. "The whole fifth grade is counting on you!"

"If they want to snoop around in Ryan Nelson's business, the whole fifth grade will have to do it themselves."

"What about Darla Wiggins?" Mandy argued. "You want *her* to win?"

No, I didn't. I definitely didn't. "I can't do anything about Darla," I told Mandy. "I just have to do what I think is right."

"But, Darcy —" Mandy tried again.

I didn't want to give her another chance to change my mind. "I have to go, Mandy," I said. "I still have homework to finish."

Math isn't my best subject, even when I don't have a mystery on my mind. I did the first problem three times. I got three different answers. I was pretty sure none of them was right.

I went downstairs to find my mother. She was a whole lot better at solving problems than I was — even if I *was* a daring detective. She was in the living room, writing a letter to Grandma and Grandpa Doyle. "I need help, Mom," I told her.

She put down her pen and tablet. I sat down next to her. "What's the problem?" she said.

I didn't know how to explain the real problem. "It's this math," I said. "Just when I get fractions figured out, Mr. Ruiz throws decimals at us!"

Mom helped me work through the first problem step-by-step. Then she watched me do the next problem and pointed out where I was going wrong. I finished the two rows Mr. Ruiz had assigned. Then Mom checked my answers. I'd only missed one problem.

Mom smiled. "See?" she said. "It's not so hard once you know what you're doing."

"Thanks, Mom." I folded the paper and put it in my book. My mother picked up her unfinished letter and started writing.

I sat for a minute and then said, "Uh, I have another problem. Harder than decimals even." She looked up, and I told her about Ryan Nelson.

"I feel terrible, Mom," I said when I was finished. "He'll probably never speak to me again!"

Mom gave me a hug. "You just keep acting like a friend. Sooner or later, you'll get through to him."

I tried acting like a friend, but it didn't go very well.

The next morning, I walked two blocks out of my way so I could walk to school with Ryan. As soon as he saw me, he went back into his house and slammed the door.

I moved my desk next to his when Miss Woodson told us to choose a partner for social studies. He shoved his desk away from me and did the worksheet by himself.

I picked him for my volleyball team in gym class. He glared at me, and then told Mr. Weis, "I'm not feeling well." He spent the rest of the period in the nurse's office.

At the end of the day, when it was time to line up and go home, Ryan was still busy finishing his language arts essay. I brought him his jacket and book bag from the cloakroom. "Keep your hands off my things!" he growled, and snatched the jacket out of my hands.

Then, after school, Ryan did something that made my jaw drop open. He ran right up to Darla Wiggins and said, "I'm ready to do that interview!"

Darla immediately looked around to make sure I was watching. She gave me a smug sort of smile and waved. Then she took out her tablet and pencil and started writing down what Ryan was telling her.

Mandy came up behind me. "Well," she said, watching Ryan talk to Darla, "I hope you're satisfied. Darla's getting the whole story. The sixth grade wins."

It didn't make sense. Why would Ryan Nelson get mad at me for trying to find out his secret, and then blab the whole thing to Darla Wiggins? "Hmmm," I said.

Mandy cocked her head sideways and grinned at me. "I thought you were off the case, Darcy J. Doyle."

I took out my own notebook and started scribbling down the clues I hadn't yet added to my list: *Living with grandmother. Goes away with mother on Saturdays. Doesn't want to talk about where they go. Talking to Darla Wiggins.*

I wished I knew what it meant. "Yeah," I told Mandy. "I thought so, too."

She pointed toward Ryan and Darla. "Well, it doesn't really matter now. Darla's getting the whole story."

I stared at my clues. "Maybe . . ."

CHAPTER 6

"Ryan Nelson's father was a hero," Darla Wiggins announced at recess the next afternoon. The whole fifth and sixth grade had gathered around her on the playground — all except Ryan, who was working on a report in the library.

"Wow!"

"Really?"

"What'd he do?"

Darla looked right at me when she told us. "He saved a bunch of little kids in a fire."

"Wow!"

"He must really be brave!"

"Why didn't Ryan want to talk about *that?* I'd be proud if it was my dad."

Darla was glad to tell us that, too. She shook her head sadly. "He died. That's why Ryan doesn't like to talk about it."

"That's too bad."

"Poor Ryan."

"How'd you find out about it, Darla?"

Darla was more than glad to explain. "It wasn't easy," she said, looking right at me again. "Only a really good investigator could have done it."

It was all I could do to keep from telling the kids exactly how much investigating Darla had done. And Darla didn't make it any easier for me.

"Well, Darcy," she said. "I guess you know what this means."

I did, but I wouldn't admit it. "I'm sure you'll tell me," I said.

She did. "It means that I'm a very good reporter." She smiled, but her smile wasn't very nice. "And you're not such a great detective after all."

The whole sixth grade grinned at me. I was a good enough detective to know what they were thinking: *Let's see you top that, Darcy J. Doyle!*

Mandy poked me in the side. "Tell her you're still on the case," she whispered in my ear.

It was tempting. The whole fifth grade was looking at me, too. And none of them were smiling. I just stood there, staring at Darla.

She laughed, loudly. "Maybe you should change your name," she suggested. "To Darcy Doyle, Defeated Detective?"

I remembered what our Sunday school

teacher, Mrs. Benson, told us about turning the other cheek. That was hard to do when both cheeks were already burning with embarrassment. "Come on," I told Mandy. "I don't want to be late for music class."

I could hear Darla Wiggins and the whole sixth grade laughing behind my back all the way to the door.

My Saturday morning baseball game wasn't much fun. I kept thinking about Ryan Nelson — and Darla Wiggins. I struck out three times. After the game, I took Max for another walk over to Kennedy Boulevard. Ryan's grandmother answered the door. The house smelled of hot apple pie. Max strained at his leash, trying to drag me inside. Good old Max, always anxious to look for more clues when a case isn't going very well.

"I'd like to see Ryan," I told Mrs. Anderson.

Max raised his nose in the air and sniffed at the spicy aroma coming from the back of the house. He drooled on the doormat. Ryan's grandmother didn't seem to mind. She bent down and gave him a couple of pats on the head. "I'm afraid Ryan isn't here, dear," she said.

I knew he went away on Saturdays, but I'd been hoping he'd be back already. I wanted to try to apologize again. I also wanted to ask him why he had changed his mind and decided to talk to Darla Wiggins. "When will he be home?" I asked.

"Oh, not until late," Mrs. Anderson answered. "They'll be in Rockville until five. Then they'll have dinner someplace. And it takes three hours to drive home." I reminded myself to add *Goes to Rockville* to my list of clues. For some reason that name sounded familiar.

"Will Ryan be home tomorrow afternoon?" I asked.

"I think so," she said. She smiled. "I think he'd like some company."

I didn't think Ryan would be all that happy to have *my* company. "Thanks," I said. "I'll see if I can come back then."

Good old Max doesn't like to give up in the middle of a case. It took all my strength to pull him down the steps. I turned to say good-bye to Mrs. Anderson. "I was really sorry to hear about Ryan's dad," I told her.

She looked surprised. "You know about Ryan's father?"

Max tried to pull me back up the steps. He knew a good clue when he heard one. "Everybody knows, Mrs. Anderson," I said. "He must have been real brave."

Her brow wrinkled in confusion. "Brave?"

"You know, saving those kids like that? In a big fire and all?" I said.

Ryan's grandmother sort of chewed at her lower lip for a few seconds. Then she closed her front door as if I wasn't even there. She didn't even say good-bye.

I was sorry I'd mentioned Ryan's father. I didn't know it would upset her so much. "Wonder what that was all about?" I asked Max. My faithful bloodhound was as curious as I was. He whined and tugged at his leash, trying to pull me back toward the house.

"Tomorrow, Max," I promised him.

We went over to Milton Park, where the ducks chased Max around the duck pond. The whole time, I thought about Ryan Nelson and the story he'd told Darla Wiggins.

As soon as I got home, I took Dad's road map out of the glove compartment of the station wagon. I looked up Rockville. I found it, but that didn't help. I went inside to get my notebook and talk to my dad. I found him down in his workshop. "You ever been to Rockville, Dad?" I asked.

He looked up from the chair leg he was tightening. "A couple of times," he told me. "Why?"

"I'm sort of working on a case," I said. "Anything special I should know about Rockville? It sounds sort of familiar."

Dad put down his screwdriver. He tried to wiggle the chair leg with his hand to see if he had it tight enough. I was pretty sure my brother Allen would get another lecture about not using the dining room chair as a rocker during dinner.

The chair leg seemed tight, and Dad smiled. "Well," he said, "there's a big corrugated box factory up there."

I wrote *box factory* in my notebook. But I didn't think Ryan would be hiding something about a box factory. Nobody would care much about boxes.

"And they have a very good community college," Dad went on.

I added *community college* to my list of clues. I didn't think that was it either. Why would anybody keep a community college a secret?

Dad tugged at the other three chair legs, one at a time, to see if they needed tightening, too. "And of course there's the Rockville State Correctional Facility."

I didn't write it down. I couldn't spell it. "The state what?" I asked.

Dad picked up his screwdriver and attacked another loose chair leg. "There's a big state prison up in Rockville, Darcy," he said.

CHAPTER 7

It took me most of Sunday afternoon to work up the courage to go back to Ryan's house. I took my faithful bloodhound with me.

As soon as we came around the corner onto Kennedy Boulevard, Max started to drool. He took off running toward Mrs. Anderson's.

When he started whining and scratching at the door, I had to knock. And when he pulled the leash out of my hand and pushed right by Mrs. Anderson, I had to follow him into the house. He galloped full speed down the hallway. Good old Max, always anxious to wrap up another big case.

I found him with Ryan in the kitchen. He was licking Ryan's face. I pulled him away. It was a struggle.

"Maybe we better take him over to the park. Before he wrecks your grandmother's kitchen," I told Ryan.

Ryan gave me an angry look. Max wouldn't leave him alone, so Ryan broke off a piece of the ham-and-cheese sandwich he was eating and tossed it to Max. My faithful bloodhound swallowed it whole. Then he looked up at Ryan with big, pitiful eyes. You'd have thought he hadn't eaten in days.

Ryan fell for it. He gave Max another bite of sandwich and scratched behind his ears. I tried giving Ryan a pitiful look, too. It didn't work nearly as well for me. "What's the matter?"

Ryan asked. "Haven't you done enough snooping for one week?"

I would have given him one of my looks, but I was trying to get him to forgive me. "I don't snoop," I told him. "I do detective work. But that's not what I was doing the time we went to the park."

Ryan wasn't convinced. "Sure," he said. "You just came over here that day because you liked me so much."

"Well, no," I admitted. "I came over to do some snoop — uh, some investigating. But I asked you to go to the park because I liked you."

He kept looking at Max, but I could tell he was weakening a little.

"I'm not here as a detective, Ryan," I said. "I'm here as a friend."

He still wasn't looking at me. Now he was

looking out the kitchen window. "I don't want you hanging around," he said.

I had a feeling I knew why. "I already know about your dad," I said.

"Sure you do," he said, "but only because I told Darla about it."

"I wasn't talking about the story you told Darla," I said.

"I don't know what you're talking about," Ryan said uneasily.

"I know about Rockville, Ryan. I know you go there to visit your father. In prison."

It had been a guess — what we daring detectives call a bluff. But one look at Ryan's face told me I was right.

It took him a few seconds before he could say anything. "I bet the kids at school will be real impressed when you tell them," he said at last.

He was right. The kids at school would be impressed. And it would make Darla Wiggins look pretty silly. The whole fifth grade would love me. But I wouldn't like myself very much. I could prove I was a really good detective. But I'd also be showing that I wasn't much of a friend.

"I'm not planning to tell them, Ryan," I said.

We talked it over while we walked Max through Milton Park. As we skipped stones across the duck pond, Ryan told me that his dad had taken some money from the company he worked for. The story had been on television and in the newspapers back in Chicago. Some of the kids at his old school had given Ryan a hard time about it.

Ryan angrily plopped a stone into the water. "Dad keeps asking me if I can ever forgive him," he said.

"Can you?" I asked him.

Ryan's last stone skimmed across the surface of the pond. "I'm trying, Darcy. He says he did it for us. And I know how sorry he is. But I still get really mad sometimes, especially when he's not here and Mom and I need him."

I told him what Pastor Jordan had said in church that morning: that God wants us to forgive others because he forgives us.

"You mean for things like telling lies about your father?" Ryan asked.

I nodded. "And for things like being a detective when you're supposed to be a friend."

He smiled. I thought it was a good sign. "While you're working on forgiving your dad, maybe you can work at forgiving me, too?" I suggested.

"Who do you have to forgive?" Ryan asked.

I thought about Darla Wiggins calling me "desperate detective" in front of Ryan Nelson.

I thought about her calling me "defeated detective" in front of the whole fifth and sixth grades. And I knew she'd rub it in for a long, long time about what a good reporter she was.

I sighed. "I guess I should start with Darla Wiggins," I said.

Ryan made a face. "Good luck!"

"Hey," I said. "A bunch of kids are going to play baseball after school on —"

Max interrupted. He raised his nose in the air and sniffed. Then he tugged at the leash so hard I nearly fell into the pond. I took a whiff too. I smiled. "Race you to the popcorn stand!" I told Ryan.

It was no contest. Max led the whole way. And he ate more than his share of the popcorn. I kept the bag for my scrapbook. As a reminder of another important case solved by Darcy J. Doyle, Daring Detective.

Catch Up on All of Darcy's Cases!

The Case of the Mixed-Up Monsters
Book 1 $2.99 0-310-57921-X

 Somebody has been making a mess in the neighborhood, and everybody thinks it's Darcy's pesky little brother. Join Darcy as she gets to the truth.

The Case of the Choosey Cheater
Book 2 $2.99 0-310-57901-5

 The big game is coming, and somebody is stealing homework. Darcy thinks the two are linked, but she doesn't have much time to solve the mystery.

The Case of the Giggling Ghost
Book 3 $2.99 0-310-57911-2

 Is Mrs. Pendleton's house really haunted? What about all those noises? It's up to Darcy to solve the mystery.

The Case of the Pampered Poodle
Book 4 $2.99 0-310-57891-4

 Fifi, the prize-winning poodle, has disappeared— right before the pet show. It takes faithful Max and a special kind of courage for Darcy to solve this case.

The Case of the Creepy Campout
Book 5 $2.99 0-310-43271-5

 When things keep going wrong on the youth group campout, everybody thinks Tricia is causing the problems. It's Darcy's job to find out the truth.

The Case of the Bashful Bully
Book 6 $2.99 0-310-43281-2

 Nobody can figure out the new boy. Nice one minute, fighting the next. What's going on? It's a race between Darcy and the snoopy school reporter to find out.

The Case of the Angry Actress
Book 7 $2.99 0-310-43301-0

 Somebody's rude "practical jokes" could stop the school play. Who is the culprit? It's up to Darcy to find an answer before the play is canceled.

The Case of the Missing Max
Book 8 $2.99 0-310-43311-8

 Vacation with Grandma and Grandpa was supposed to be fun, but instead Darcy is frantic. Her faithful dog, Max, has disappeared!